DEVIL'S DOORSTEP

Weekly Reader Children's Book Club
presents

DEVIL'S DOORSTEP

MARIAN RUMSEY

ILLUSTRATED BY W. T. MARS

William Morrow and Company
New York

For Tom, my other son.

Weekly Reader Children's Book Club Edition
Intermediate Division

CONTENTS

‖1‖

TORNADO ARRIVES

Every summer Peter Burke, who was ten years old, went to Devil's. Doorstep. Devil's Doorstep was a mountain over two miles high. From its summit Peter could see to the east, west, north, and south—hundreds of miles of never-ending land. Almost every day Peter went to the pinnacle, his favorite spot, the very highest point of Devil's Doorstep. There he sat and read, or just gazed into the vastness of the great Rocky Mountains.

Peter's father was a fire watcher. He was contented at Devil's Doorstep Station, so he had returned to the lookout each season for almost eight years. The family lived in a small cabin, which Peter's father and mother had built when they first came to Devil's. But that was long ago. Peter had grown in spurts like a sapling pine. His hair was dark, his eyes the color of the tall blue sky. He was thin, wiry, and very strong.

One day in August Peter was waiting to see the helicopter. It brought mail and supplies, and his new assortment of library books. But the only thing in sight was a bird, a hawk probably, soaring to the east, then back, in an effortless glide. He wondered idly if some unsuspecting, small animal would appear, and the bird would have its meal. He hoped not. Peter had many animal friends in the mountains, and though he had learned long ago life in the animal kingdom was harsh and brutal, he did not want blood spilled on such a lovely morning.

Then he heard it. At first a soft whirring, followed by a deeper puffing and pumping. Peter leaped from his special place and ran, skidding frantically down the shale and loose stones, sending them scudding over and over to tumble into the chasm below. He streaked down the path lined with hay-colored bracken and buckwheat, and stumbled slightly as he reached the tower.

"It's coming!" he shrieked. Father was already on the tower porch, hands on his hips looking to the north. Mother came out the cabin door, her knitting in her hands. She tossed it on the porch chair and ran with Peter. The sound of the helicopter was now almost overpowering. Ahead they could see the sudden waving of the trees from the wind as it splayed them apart, and the clear air became filled with the white

seeds of some mountain plant. Startled birds
flew in every direction. The mule snorted, ran
sharply this way and that, and laid back her ears.
Then abruptly the noise ceased, and Peter heard
Father shouting at Bill Price, the pilot.

Peter ran to the little shelter down the slope,
where they kept their white mule, Dolly. He
vaulted the corral fence and snatched Dolly's
halter. After years of practice and experience,
he and Mother were able to saddle the mule

quickly with her pack. While Mother held back
the rail, Peter ran Dolly out and down the path
to the meadow. Peter left her lead very long, and
Dolly staunchly trotted at her own determined
speed.

[15]

Father had already run ahead and was now ducking under the rotor. Bill jumped out, and there was much shaking of hands and slapping of shoulders. Mother received a big hug and a bundle of mail, and Peter continued to call Dolly such unbearable names as Worm, Sluggard, and Lazy Cow, for not hurrying.

No one in the family would dream of leaving Devil's Doorstep for the outside, but what fun it was to have a visitor, especially Bill Price with his thick gray hair, his sharp dark eyes, and warm laugh. The supplies were unloaded —groceries, meat, books, and those special little things a person misses when the nearest city is two hundred miles away. As they loaded Dolly, Father discussed the family's light generator troubles and spoke cautious words about the dryness of the timber. All the while Peter climbed in and out of the helicopter like a nervous fly that could never light. Only Dolly was uninterested and kicked one hoof at her harness from sheer habit.

Soon everyone stopped talking, and Bill looked at Peter with a twinkle in his eye. "How's life on Devil's Doorstep?" he asked Peter.

Peter grinned.

"Good, eh. How would you like a friend to stay with you awhile?"

"You?" asked Peter happily. What fun it would be to have Bill and his helicopter there all the time.

He shook his head. "How can I supply other stations or keep a fire watch, if you keep me here. No, this is a young man."

Peter eyed Bill warily. He knew the jokes the pilot liked to play, and somehow he wondered if this friend was one of them.

Bill put his hand on Peter's head. "He's around the other side."

[17]

"What?" said Peter foolishly, and ran around the helicopter. He had seen no one since Bill landed. "Oh, you're joking, there's no one here."

"Yes there is, right there."

Peter looked at the crate strapped to the outside of the plane and frowned. Certainly no person could fit in that, or if he could, what an odd place to have put him. The front was screened, and Peter knelt to look inside. It was shadowy, and suddenly there came a quick scrambling and a loud bleating.

Peter laughed. "What is it? A sheep?"

Bill unlatched the cage front and took down a length of rope. As he did so a small head popped out, and Bill immediately collared it with the line.

"A goat!" said Peter happily. "It's a baby goat!"

The goat scrambled nimbly down to the

[18]

ground. He looked so tiny and so sturdy standing there that everyone laughed. He was black with some white and tan. His eyes were dark, fringed with long lashes, and he had lanky ears that flapped in the breeze. Two tiny, nubby horns made him look just a bit devilish.

"I was supposed to fly him out and turn him loose. A sheepherder gave him to the Admundsens at Eagle's Peak Station a few months ago." Bill cleared his throat. "He got into things some, and they didn't want him anymore. They tried turning him loose, but he always came back."

Peter took the rope and knelt beside the little animal.

"His name's Tornado," offered Bill half-apologetically.

"Tornado!"

"The Admundsens wanted me to ask you folks if you might like him for a pet."

[21]

"Oh, yes!" said Peter happily.

"Now wait a minute," said Mother solemnly. "Bill, is there any other reason why the Admundsens want him away from Eagle's Peak Station?"

"Well, he likes to climb, and they were afraid he might get hurt. You know how Anna Admundsen is, always afraid of an animal's getting hurt."

Peter put his arms around the little goat. Tornado sniffed his neck, then began to scratch his young horns against his arm. Somehow Peter didn't think Tornado was free of faults. At least, Bill was talking awfully fast, and that glint of devilishness in Tornado's eyes could mean many things. He grinned. "Mother, please let him stay. If he isn't good, Bill can take him away next month when he stops with supplies."

"Splendid idea," said Bill, slapping Peter on the back.

They all walked to the cabin. Mother had baked a blueberry pie, and the steaming coffee on the stove smelled delicious. Peter sat outside on the steps, listening halfheartedly, as Father went over the list for next month and they checked reports. Mother cut more pie. Peter found Tornado liked pie very much, and so they shared it. But it became very obvious that the sharing came from Peter, for he was left with the crust.

"I always stay longer than I plan," said Bill, shaking Father's hand later. "Don't forget, any problems and I can be here in an hour. Providing, of course, there is a pie waiting for me." He twinkled at Mother. The family stood back, while the rotors began to move, whine, then roar. The plane lifted, slowly at first, and everyone waved. Bill grinned happily at them, and then the plane went up like a shot. In a moment he was over the trees and gone.

[23]

"Goodness," said Mother, "like a whirlwind, that whirlybird man."

Father shook Peter's shoulder. "Better put Tornado in the corral with Dolly, and then take a stand on duty. I want to work on the generator."

So together Tornado and Peter went to Dolly's lean-to. Tornado was quite happy to be trotting after Peter on the end of his lead. He seemed perfectly at home with the boy. In fact, either because of the pie or perhaps because he was looking for a little friendship, Tornado seemed quite fond of Peter.

Peter opened the corral gate, loosened the line from Tornado's neck, and patted him gently on the head. "Now see if you and Dolly can get along." And with that he threw the rope over the fence and ran for the tower steps.

|| 2 ||

THE FIRST NIGHT

It was always fun to have the duty, as Father called it. Then Peter felt responsible for the hundreds of miles of timber around him. Peering over the tower porch rail, he saw Father uncover the generator motor behind the cabin. It supplied power for the radio, but was a balky brute, as stubborn toward work as their mule Dolly. Mother had started the stove, and a puff of smoke belched out the stone chimney. Dinner was probably in the offing. The thought of smoke sent Peter inside the tower to get to work.

His first glance was to the south, where he might catch a last glimpse of Bill's helicopter. He used Father's binoculars, but saw no sign of it. Automatically he turned the radio switch on, and the light flashed red. The transmission was open now, and if there was a call from the other stations he would hear the ring.

The closest station was the Admundsens' on Eagle's Peak to the north. With the glasses Peter picked out the outline of a tower. Eagle's Peak was a wicked place, and Father worried about the Admundsens on windy nights in the late fall. The mountain was sheer and steep above timberline, even rockier than Devil's, and the tower clutched the top of it like an ugly, long-legged bug.

Peter swung the glasses around the horizon, but saw no smoke. It was very dry, so dry that the timber crackled. If the weather report earlier had been right, they were due for rain—a good thing. Father said the fire hazard was grave. It was so extreme, in fact, that both Mother and Father had been sleeping less and less each night and making their checks more and more often.

Just for fun Peter decided to check a position on the firefinder. Being a little short, he stood on a stool in front of the tall lens to see better. It was not easy to pick out a spot in the distant valley in the scope. Taking his time, he looked across the trees with his naked eye, then spotted the same area in the hairline lens. Once done, he noted the number of degrees on a card and transferred the reading to the master map. With the protractor he found the exact bearing from Devil's Doorstep.

Picking up the binoculars, Peter made another sweep around the horizon. Suddenly a curtain of black blotted out his field of vision. He blinked his eyes, put down the glasses, and sucked in his breath with a gasp.

That black blob was Tornado. He was nonchalantly standing on the narrow wooden railing that circled the tower porch. Peter was afraid that if he went out the door to snatch the little goat, the animal might suddenly become frightened and fall backward sixty feet to the ground. Peter ran his tongue over his lips. "Tornado," he whispered.

The goat watched him through the glass. He had been lonely and had searched out his new friend.

"Tornado, you idiot," said Peter foolishly. "Come here!" At that the goat jumped down from the narrow rail and pranced to the door. Peter let him in, threw his arms around his neck, and held him tightly. Tornado rubbed his horns on his leg, and Peter sighed in relief.

[28]

That evening Peter locked Tornado in the fire equipment shed. Obviously it would be useless to put him in the corral again, since he could climb out so easily. Not more than ten minutes had passed when a loud clattering sent the family running out to the shed.

"What is that goat doing in there?" said Father irritably.

Peter rushed to the shed door and eased it open, only to leap back with a scream. A black bullet, head down and horns forward, charged toward him with the speed of a locomotive. Peter flung himself safely out of the way just as Tornado hit the unlocked door, sending it back with a crash. Then he skidded to a stop, surveying his audience with a loud bleat and slightly shaking his head. He trotted to Peter who was lying flat on the ground.

"Good heavens!" said Father furiously. "He's broken the hinges!"

[29]

"What about his head?" said Peter tenderly.
However, Tornado nibbled Peter's sleeve happily and seemed perfectly all right.

"Head be hanged," said Father fuming. "It's
the door I'm thinking about."

What to do with Tornado for the night suddenly became a problem. Father would not risk
putting the little goat back into the shed. Be-

sides butting the door into shreds, he might damage the fire equipment that was essential to the safety of the timber.

"Tie him up," he told Peter shortly.

Peter had more sense than to disobey. He could hear Mother mentioning the Admundsens, and Peter was somewhat afraid Tornado, in his first few hours as guest, had just about overstayed his welcome.

He looked around for a good place to tie the animal. His lead was long, and it would give him plenty of freedom. He heard Mother and Father slamming the door of the tower as they went back to work. Peter arranged the crate from the helicopter by the porch. At least Tornado could sleep inside it for the night. He tied the line to one of the porch logs, patted the little goat, and went inside.

Just as Peter got into bed he heard a clatter at the window. There was Tornado on the sill,

[31]

scraping his horns on the screen. Peter leaped out of bed, shouted, and the goat jumped down. Grumbling, he closed the shutters and resigned himself to a hot night. He could hear the little goat exploring. Tornado had apparently no intention of sleeping in his crate, but preferred the comfort of the porch. There was a sharp rattle, then silence, a crash, and more silence. What *was* he doing?

Finally Peter slipped out of bed, quietly opened the shutters, and looked out. The moon was waxing full and had just come up. But where was the silly goat? He leaned farther out the window, shook his head, and reclosed the screen. No need going back to bed until he knew exactly where the goat had settled for the night. Opening the front door, Peter noticed he hadn't shut it as well as he thought. He felt something under his feet, knelt down, and saw it was Tornado's rope.

[32]

Peter hurried back to the table and lit the kerosene lamp. "Oh, no!"

There was Tornado, perched precariously on top of the kitchen sink, reaching and stretching his front feet to the highest shelf. He had already demolished all the bread Mother had spent the day baking. The sugar bowl was tipped over—so was the coffee can. The sticky stuff on the floor was the syrup, and the potato bin had been heavily depleted. Just then Tornado nudged the cracker box from the shelf and began tearing at the paper.

"You!" scolded Peter. He took the animal by the collar, but since Tornado was not anxious to leave, he sat down and had to be dragged. At last Peter got him outside and began cleaning up the mess. Father would be in to make coffee at midnight and things had better be put away neatly. Then came a clatter of hooves and a sudden cabin-shattering crash.

[33]

The door shook, spewed out dust and splinters, and resettled on its hinges.

Peter sat in the nearest chair. Surely one little goat would be unable to break down the front door! Another jarring crash, another clattering of little hooves! Time after time the door shook, creaked, and settled solidly back in place. Hearing Father shout from the tower, Peter opened the door and looked at Tornado shaking his head slightly, ready for his next charge. Peter reassured Father and spoke to Tornado solemnly. "You silly goat," he said sternly, but had to laugh. Tornado was rubbing against his leg affectionately. That was why Peter let the goat into the cabin while he cleaned, swept, and neatly closed all shelf doors.

Finally Peter called Tornado to his room. After Tornado jumped to the dresser top, the window sill, and the top of the bedside table, he climbed to the foot of Peter's bed. Bending

[34]

his front knees, the goat knelt, then lay on the bed. He looked at Peter, opened his mouth, and said his good-night. At least Peter thought that the loud, lip-lifting babble meant good-night in goat language.

‖3‖

FOREST LIFE

The friendship that grew between the boy and the goat was fun for both of them. Tornado had an insatiable curiosity, and Peter an understanding heart. After all Peter was a youngster himself. He could understand Tornado's need for exploring, poking his nose into things of no concern to him, and even his desire to climb.

Mother scolded Peter about letting the goat into the cabin. So in the evenings Peter had to lock Tornado out. Each time the goat became incensed, furious that he was separated from the boy who had become his everlasting friend. If Peter tied him to the cabin, Tornado only began an unending attack on the door or wall and scrambled noisily around the porch until it was impossible for anyone to sleep.

Peter then tried to tie him in the corral with Dolly, but it soon was apparent that Dolly and Tornado would never accept each other. The braying and bleating that came from the corral even reached Father in the tower. Tornado refused to stay on the ground, preferring to walk on the wooden corral rail or even climb onto the lean-to roof. Dolly grew nervous and sulky. She was further upset when Tornado refused to eat standing in front of the feedbox like a normal animal. Instead he perched unsteadily on its narrow rim, tipped almost upside-down. And Tornado ate Dolly's food at that, as if he were starving! Dolly had a right to snort, bray,

and kick her heels furiously at her tormentor.

Peter then tried tying Tornado to a short, small tree near the cabin. But Tornado attacked it with such energy that the pine cones dropped all around like bombs. At last Peter removed the goat to an older pine tree, and despite the butting it took, it never wavered an inch. In fact, by morning, the little goat lay exhausted and sleepy at the end of his tether, staring balefully at the tree. A trampled path of dry grass ringed the old tree like a halo.

In the morning Peter always untied him and fed him his own share of feed away from Dolly. Then he let him roam wherever he wished. Possibly insuring himself against losing Peter, Tornado followed the boy like a puppy. He clattered along on cloven hooves, his short tail turned up and his beginning billy-goat beard twitching.

One morning the boy, the goat, and the mule wandered for miles, always within sight of the tower. They circled endlessly in the thick timber along the slopes. It was an old growth, and here and there huge giants had died, fallen, and left their remains to decay and turn to dust. At one of these fallen trees Peter stopped to rest and to watch the little things using it as a haven.

Termites were busily honeycombing the log, making it look like Swiss cheese. Bees hummed around its one remaining spiral of twisted and decayed trunk. Perhaps there was a hive hidden in its rotten core. A chipmunk stood rod straight and surveyed his home with a nervous chatter; his tail signaled disapproval of the group ringed about the fallen pine. A woodpecker flew to the standing trunk and seemed to be sucked inside through a tiny hole. From his nest he turned about and peered intently at Tornado nibbling a fresh green vine. High overhead sliver-thin threads of spider webs stretched toward the sun.

Peter stepped on the log so he could jump onto Dolly's back. "Come along," he said, and Dolly pricked up her ears. They made their way to the tiny creek that wound down from the top of Devil's. It was dry now, filled with stones.

[42]

Suddenly there came the clatter of larger hooves on stone. Tornado reared on his back legs as two deer crossed the boulders to the other side of the stream bed directly in front of him. Peter held his breath. Dolly, her ears rotating like periscopes, watched the deer as closely as Tornado. One was a big buck with a large set of antlers. The other was a doe and much smaller. Tornado immediately clambered across the stream bed and began to follow them. Hurrying, the deer disappeared into the thick, dry cover, Tornado still hot in pursuit of his quarry.

The buck turned back to see what sort of creature was coming after them. He waited until Tornado was within a stone's throw, then showed himself completely. Peter felt a sudden touch of fear. He knew the danger of those horns. Tornado, however, knew only that this animal was more like himself than like Dolly.

[43]

After all, he had no reason to think of danger. In fact, in all his young life Tornado had never known danger.

The buck allowed the goat to come no closer. He ducked his head and made a sweep and feint with his antlers. From pure amazement Tornado stopped. The buck stepped closer, eyed the goat with a menacing glare, and hooked at him again. Tornado stared at his odd performance. The buck stepped closer and Peter bit his lip.

"Tornado!" he called sharply. Dolly brayed noisily. The buck looked at them sullenly and disappeared into the underbrush. Tornado ran for Peter and Dolly, considering his encounter with the strange animals over. Peter breathed more easily and was glad when they sighted the corral. Dolly was lagging noticeably by this time, probably ready for her mid-morning nap.

This experience should have been enough

[46]

for one day, but later that afternoon Father called from the tower. "Bears," he said to Peter.

Bears were not uncommon on Devil's Doorstep. Occasionally one might pay a visit to the station, but not often. These two were on the

[47]

edge of the clearing. One was black and quite large; the other was cinnamon. Although neither were adult bears, they were both large enough for Peter. He had a great respect for bears and gave them a wide berth.

"Mother has been frying bacon," said Father, coming down the steps. "They can't resist that smell."

But they were not ready to come any closer. Peter heard Mother shutting the door of the tower. She hated bears. Father closed the cabin door and the shutters, and he and Peter were ready to watch the hesitant animals. But they had forgotten Tornado. He pranced around the cabin, with his head high, and jauntily came up to investigate the new smell.

"Good grief!" said Father, stunned.

"Tornado!" shouted Peter frantically.

"You fool goat," said Father, half-fearfully. "Come back here!"

[48]

"Peter," called Mother from the tower window. "What is that goat doing?"

"Tornado!" screeched Peter.

But the two nervous bears were not interested in a fidgety goat. It was courageous of them to have ventured near the human smell. Unlike the bears of the National Parks that have become so tame as to be a nuisance, these bears were ignorant of man. They knew only that human beings were different from animals of their forest and should be treated cautiously. But the smell of the frying bacon had been an overpowering magnet. As Tornado approached them, the bears turned to leave, their gait deliberate and misleadingly ponderous. Pointedly, they ignored Tornado.

The family knew very well the danger that had hovered about Tornado. Father spoke stern words to Peter, and Mother shook her head in dismay. Peter realized Tornado must

[49]

learn his place in the forest life or he would certainly come to harm.

The next morning dawned very hot. Father began the day by nervously watching the hygrometer. Once the humidity reached sixty per cent or below at sunrise, it became fire weather —and it had been near that this morning.

Peter walked the animals for their exercise toward the deeper trees. It was a little cooler there, but still almost stifling. The birds sang in spurts as if it was too hot to bother. Perhaps that long-overdue rain would come soon.

They stopped. Peter slipped off Dolly's back and stood ankle-deep in the dry grass. Tornado nibbled one of the smaller bushes. He sampled just about everything in hopes that it might be edible. Suddenly a stranger appeared beside him. It was a skunk, her stripe vividly white against her black coat. The meeting was unexpected, and the skunk was slightly startled.

[50]

Nevertheless, she knew the forest animals and assuming that, as always, she would be left alone, she deliberately made her way along the path. Tornado looked down his Roman-shaped nose at her with interest. The skunk stopped and

snuffled at the fallen leaves. Temptation, Tornado's downfall, gripped him.

Peter knew instantly that the little goat was preparing to charge. His head came down, those nubby little horns dipped, and he ran full tilt at the skunk.

The skunk released her spray with all her might. She wasn't hurt, though Tornado sent her plunging in unladylike fashion into a bush.

"Oh, no," said Peter, holding his nose. For once Tornado was shaking his head with cause. He couldn't stand the smell himself. He ran in circles, bleating, and then came to Peter for help. Dolly reared and balked. The goat rubbed against Peter's leg, trying to tell him that the situation was terrible.

"Whew!" groaned Peter, hurrying to the stump to mount Dolly. "Don't touch me."

And it was a very smelly threesome that arrived back at the tower.

[52]

"Peter," said Father helplessly, "get that goat away from here."

Unhappily, it became Peter's job to give Tornado a bath. Putting him into the big tub by the water tank was hard enough, but trying to hold him in it and still launder him with the brush was even more difficult. When he finished, Peter was soaked and exhausted, as well as covered with soap and goat hairs. Tornado shook himself and started to roll in the dust, but Peter caught him just in time.

"Put him in the fire shed," said Father. "I suppose it will be all right for tonight."

"Silly goat," said Peter sympathetically. "Have you learned your lesson about skunks?"

"I rather doubt it," said Father, laughing despite himself. Peter shut him in the shed, expecting momentarily to hear a loud, shattering bash. But, strangely enough, there was silence.

[55]

||4||

DOWN THE MOUNTAIN

Peter's father discovered the reason for Tornado's silence the next morning. When he came into the cabin, his face was grave and his glasses were pushed high on his forehead.

"What is it?" asked Mother quickly.

Father had a fire extinguisher in his hand. "I've been to the fire shed," he said quietly. He put the cylinder on the table. "Peter," he said unhappily, "look at this."

"The label's off," Peter said quickly. He

knew that every single thing in the fire shed was always labeled.

Father sighed. "That goat spent the night in the shed licking every label from every size tin in there."

Peter swallowed.

"Peter, you realize what this means. I happen to know which label belongs on which tin. But if I didn't, think what might happen."

"But why did Tornado do it?" said Mother. "Surely he's fed well enough not to want to eat paper."

"Oh," said Father, "he didn't eat the labels." He handed a sticky wad of white to Peter. "He licked them because he likes the taste of the glue." He sat down beside the boy. "That isn't all. He's been licking and chewing on the fire hose. You realize what would happen if he put a leak in it. It's a high-pressure hose."

"Oh, no!" said Mother. "Is it damaged?"

[57]

"I'm going to test it out now," Father said. "If it is, I'll have to call Bill Price and have him fly out with another three coils."

"Three!" said Peter stunned. "You mean he chewed all three coils?"

Father nodded solemnly. "Peter, you know the goat will have to go. He's a hazard. I'm sorry. If it were any other time but now, when the fire weather is on, I might see another way out for him. As it is, we must get rid of him."

Peter put his head in his hands. Tornado had certainly got into trouble this time. Father was right, very right. And Peter knew he must do something he would hate.

"What should Peter do with him?" asked Mother.

Father sighed. "He'll have to take him far away from Devil's Doorstep and leave him. In the forest he can do no more damage than— than butt a skunk."

[58]

"But Father, what about bears?"

"Once Tornado is on his own he'll be much too interested in filling his fat stomach to make a nuisance of himself."

"Oh, Father," moaned Peter. "I can't take him out into the wilderness and just *leave* him."

"Yes, you can, Peter. He's dangerous. He threatens this mountaintop as much as a bundle of dynamite. Heaven knows what he may eat or chew next."

"Oh, Father!"

"Peter, I'm ordering you."

"But I love him. He's my friend."

Father put his hand on Peter's shoulder. "I know that. But would you take a chance with this timber? No, I didn't think so. Now don't feed him this morning. When you leave him, he'll want to stay and graze because he'll be hungry. Then you must get out of sight and come back a different way."

[59]

Peter nodded. He knew Father was only doing what had to be done. There was nothing Peter could do to help his little friend.

"You'll have to take him all the way down the mountain. It's a long way, and you had better start."

"I'll make you a little lunch," said Mother. She knew how Peter felt.

"No," said Peter miserably. "I'd rather not. I'll just take a candy bar and a jug of water. That will make me hurry."

"Good boy," said Father.

But Peter did not feel good—in fact, he felt awful. He rode Dolly at a fast clip down the mountainside, going faster than Dolly wanted and faster than Tornado, at the end of a lead, had planned on. Loud, unhappy noises were coming from him, and Dolly kept laying her ears flat in objection. Silly little goat. He hadn't known the damage he was doing, but all the same it had spelled disaster. Peter refused to think of the many, many things that could happen to a young goat alone in the forest. His chances would be very small. There were mountain lions, though he had never seen one, and bears, and coyotes—so many menacing enemies.

Once Tornado sat determinedly on his haunches. The line tightened against Dolly's side. "Come on, Tornado," said Peter softly. "I know you're hungry. I know you hate the rope and that you are unhappy. But Tornado, you have to get to the bottom of the mountain before I can let you go."

So they pushed ahead, never hesitating, not letting the little goat bend his head for a moment to graze. Peter felt worse all the time. The sun was hot, and the path under Dolly's feet sent up clouds of dust that made him sneeze.

Peter had not made many trips to the bottom

of Devil's Doorstep. Usually one or two times a season he would venture down to Devil's Creek to spend the day fishing for trout. But that was in the early spring when the creek ran full as a river and the fish were fat. Now the stream would be small, though the ponds made by the beavers would still be filled. Perhaps he could find a grassy meadow, one still green in the swampland, for his friend. But they were still far from the bottom, and it was going to be a fight all the way. He lifted the line from Dolly's back, so she would not be hurt by its cut.

Devil's Doorstep—what a good name for the mountain this day. It seemed to Peter that he was truly going to have to leave his friend at the devil's own doorstep. No one knew why the mountain was named as it was. Perhaps trappers or Indians of long ago had lost their friends or even families there. Possibly they

[64]

found the forest and mountain so far from home that it seemed the very end of nowhere.

If only there was some way to keep Tornado. But he could not tie the animal too far from the lookout. His blatting and babbles would attract all the hunting animals. Tornado must be free to run from enemies he might see. Peter sighed. The goat was weaving back and forth, in and out, around Dolly's feet impeding her progress down the mountain.

It would not do any good to build a corral for him this far from the cabin. Tornado would never tolerate a fence and would climb any that he built. Besides, it would be impossible to ride down every day to feed him. Peter wished he and Tornado were sitting in his special place on the pinnacle. He wished Tornado had not licked the labels from the cans, chewed at the fire hose, butted the doors, climbed the roof, teetered on rails, or eaten precious vegetables.

How could one silly little spaniel-eared beast have so many faults?

They reached the bottom of the mountain. Dolly sighed, blew, and twisted her head to watch Tornado. Even she seemed to know that this day was different from others.

"Come on," urged Peter, crossing the little-used fire trail and entering the deep forest. "We have to keep going."

They trudged along, beating their way through low brush and small trees, farther and farther from Devil's Doorstep. A small creek with leaves floating on its surface crossed their path. They forded it, Tornado balking and howling his impatience. Deeper into the trees they rode, past landmarks that he knew, on to rocky outcroppings that he did not. Finally he stopped at a place where the underbrush was dense and green.

Peter slipped from Dolly's back and took the

line from Tornado. The goat was eager to taste the new leaves and grass. He was starving, but first came to brush his head against Peter's leg. Peter threw his arms around the goat and held him. "Don't be afraid," he whispered, expecting for all the world that Tornado would understand. Then he stood up quickly, biting his lip, and watched Tornado prance to the nearest bracken and begin daintily to eat his breakfast.

Slowly, with great care, Peter mounted Dolly, turned her, and walked away. If Tornado glanced after him, Peter stopped and began adjusting Dolly's harness or examining the tallest tree overhead. Then, with a lump in his throat, he kicked Dolly in the side and they bolted out of sight.

He and Dolly ran until the mule laid back her ears in protest. Peter listened for a rustle of leaves or a crack of a branch. But there was no sound. However, he had not gone far when

[67]

Dolly rotated her ears and Peter looked back. "Oh, no." There was Tornado, frisking and prancing through the trees, catching up with them.

He put the line around Tornado's neck and began the tedious progress of taking the goat once more into the thicker trees. Again Peter attempted to leave him, only to have Tornado eventually reappear saucy as ever.

"This is great!" said Peter, half-angrily. "You must stay, you little beast."

Three times Peter left him, and always Tornado found him. But the fourth time Peter crisscrossed his trail, twisting and winding deeper and deeper into the forest. Peter knew it was nearly noon. He was hungry, and the goat must be starving. Even old Dolly needed a cool drink of water. He circled and recircled, like a spider spinning its web, until at last he found a marshy spot damp and green.

This time Tornado, tired and lagging, began to graze in earnest, and Peter slipped away easily. After minutes had passed without an appearance, or loud bleatings, he was sure he had at last made his escape. He had not realized how difficult it was to leave a goat in the forest.

‖ 5 ‖

LOST!

It was some time before Peter knew that something was wrong. At first he only frowned and turned Dolly slightly. But after a few more minutes he began to feel the perspiration roll down his forehead, and he wiped it away nervously with his hand. He turned Dolly again, then again. At last he stopped. He sat like a stone, staring at the tips of Dolly's ears.

Finally Peter looked overhead to find the sun, but it was lost in a maze of branches and only a smattering of sunshine sprinkled through. He slipped from Dolly's back and put his head against her shoulder. "Dolly," he mumbled, "do you know the way home?"

In his desire to lose Tornado, Peter had lost himself. The familiar landmarks were gone. The duff and cover here were firm, and no tracks showed. Looking about for the rise of Devil's Doorstep was useless; he would never be able to see more than a few hundred yards through the heavy timber.

"Dolly," he said again, "Dolly you are my hope, you know. Let's go home."

The mule looked at Peter pleasantly, then lowered her head to nibble the brown, dry cover under her feet.

"Home!" said Peter shrilly. "Go home!"

Dolly looked up. Peter's voice was nervous and jittery. She had no idea what he was talking about.

[71]

"Dolly!" cried Peter, jerking her harness frantically. "Dolly, we're lost! You're a mule. Can't you find your way back to the corral?"

Dolly rotated her ears and looked behind her.

"That way?" said Peter, trying not to be frightened. "Is that the way home?"

But Dolly only dipped her head again to nibble and blow the grass. She was very hungry by now.

"Come on," said Peter impatiently. "We'll try that way." He turned the mule around, then tied the long lead to her reins. He made soft clicking noises and slapped her lightly on the rump. "Go home, Dolly. Home!"

The mule walked away, glanced back at Peter holding the long lead, and stopped.

"Go home!" shouted Peter, stamping his foot.

Dolly moved ahead, and Peter felt his heart skip hopefully. Surely she would find her way.

She would know where her feedbox was. But after a few minutes it became obvious to Peter that Dolly did not know her way home any more than he. Dolly walked from one grazing spot to another without the slightest idea of where she was going.

Peter became terribly frightened. He mounted Dolly and kicked his heels in her side, making her jump in surprise. They ran, past trees that all looked the same, across stream beds, through brush that scratched and clawed at them. But it was no use. Peter stopped and put his face against Dolly's warm neck. Father had always told him that if he got lost he was to sit down quietly and wait for someone to find him. He must not run and lose himself completely, which is what he most certainly had done now.

Peter slipped down from Dolly, wrapped her line around a tree, and let her graze in peace. Poor old Dolly. She must be confused and hungry. Peter sat down on a fallen log. He was not frightened now. That first moment, when his bearings had been shaken and he had run, was the worst. He knew he was safe enough. He knew Father would find him. It would just take time. In fact, he might have to spend the night sitting right here on the old log. He hated to think of the scolding he would get from his parents. He put his chin in his hand and rolled his eyes. What a mess!

But he certainly would not move now. He was in a slight clearing, more open and meadowlike. The sun dribbled through overhead. Peter frowned. That was strange—the sun was not so bright now. Surely it wasn't getting near sundown yet. But wait—the sprinkling of light had turned to gold again. Clouds! The sun was going behind clouds. That meant the weather was changing. Peter felt better already. If it rained, Father would be able to come for him.

Suddenly Peter sucked in his breath with horror. A warm snout snuffled down his neck, his back hair was nibbled, then he felt an affectionate nip at his ear.

"Tornado!" roared Peter rapturously. "Oh, Tornado, how wonderful!" He squeezed the little goat with all his might, and Tornado wiggled in pleasure. "I guess," said Peter half-laughing, "I did my job a little too well."

Tornado pranced around the stump and went to investigate Dolly's grass. There was a sudden grumbling of personalities, and Tornado ran back to Peter, who giggled. At least, Tornado had not lost any of his devilishness.

Tornado dipped his head and butted a dry sliver of weed, then nipped it neatly in two and began to chew.

Peter laughed again. "Silly goat. Well—finish eating it. You look a little foolish with it stuck on your lip." Peter laughed again, then

[77]

sobered. Tornado was looking to one side, his beard ruffled slightly in the light air. Peter glanced at Dolly. She, too, was looking in the same direction as Tornado. Both the animals were still as statues.

Peter plucked the weed from Tornado's mouth. Tornado looked at Peter sharply, then back to what had originally held his interest. Dolly turned quickly and trotted across to the end of her lead. It stopped her abruptly, and she turned to peer over her shoulder again. Bleating noisily, Tornado raised his nose in the air and stared into the deeper woods.

Peter felt the hair on his neck tickle and stand out. These silly animals were going to get him all upset again. He stood up quickly and went to soothe Dolly. She was very tense, her eyes bright. Peter spoke to her gently. As he ran his hand down her haunches he felt her shiver.

Peter tried to make out a shape, a form in the maze of trees. He knew of no animal that would hurt them. There were bears certainly, but they were leary of man, and it was unlikely that he would see one. Yet he felt that sudden clutching of fear again. It was strange. There was no sound, nothing. The bird that had been trilling sleepily was quiet. Even the hum of bees and the faint waft of breeze had stopped. It was as if the world were standing still. His hand half-raised to stroke Dolly, Peter froze like a piece of granite.

Could it possibly be a grizzly? That breed of bear was a killer and would not confine his meals to berries, or fish, or a smaller animal. A young goat or mule might tempt one into becoming a dreadful danger. But surely a grizzly would not be here! Seldom, if ever, were any of these animals ever sighted or reported in the forest.

[79]

What, then, was hypnotizing the mule and goat? And what was causing Dolly to fidget nervously? Somehow Dolly's being upset frightened Peter even more than discovering that he had lost himself in the trees.

And then suddenly their world came alive. Peter stared in amazement. There from the bushes ran a fat raccoon, and hot on its heels another, and then another. They were followed by a sudden eruption of quail, at least twenty,

which skittered out of the brush and ran in jagged, zigzag fashion, helter-skelter in the same direction as the bandit-faced raccoons.

Peter looked at Tornado, but he was still absorbed in the trees ahead. Dolly paced anxiously to the end of her lead and back. Peter frowned. Two deer appeared. Running, first one way, then another, they disappeared with a hasty look behind them. Again Peter felt that clutching of fear. The deer hadn't been looking at him, at the mule, or at the goat—but from where they had come.

Birds began to fly overhead, making noises that caught Peter's attention. Surely that racket was not singing. He cocked his head to listen. The sound was one of irritation or anger. There was a big horned owl flying high in the treetops.

Peter frowned again. The owl and the raccoons were night animals. For them to be out this time of day was unusual, if not unheard of.

[81]

Suddenly Tornado bleated shrilly. Another deer darted into view and came toward them as if bewildered. Never hesitating, the deer passed over Dolly's lead, making her jump in terror. Peter backed against the stump, staring at the disappearing animal.

What was happening? Now came a skunk, its tail high. Peter clutched Tornado, but the goat's eyes were riveted ahead. Then three more deer bolted before them, weaving through the brush. Dolly began to bray, but the deer never glanced at her. Overhead came the thrash of wings. Birds flew through the tree branches, flailing them with their bodies. Another skunk went by—so did a squirrel and another deer. Birds screeched and cawed. Peter wiped his tongue over his lips. A chipmunk darted partly up a tree, changed his mind, skittered down, and ran behind the disappearing procession.

"What on earth?" said Peter aloud. "What is

go—" he stopped. His eyes widened, and he took another hesitant, almost unwanted breath. The very lightest smell of smoke touched his senses. He shivered uncontrollably. Smoke meant fire. Fire must be the reason for this sudden, frantic effort of the animals to leave the forest.

Quickly Peter untied Dolly. Instinctively he knew that he, too, must flee for his life. He slithered on Dolly, and without urging she began her quickest trot. Tornado bleated noisily and took his position ahead of them. But they were slower than the birds above, slower than the deer, the elk, and even the dark-coated moose with his bulbous nose. Some were walking briskly, some running, some weaving erratically, glassy-eyed with fear.

Peter snatched a glance behind him. There was nothing yet in sight, no sign of flames, no sign of smoke. There was another skunk,

[83]

though, and a squirrel, and another raccoon so fat that he could barely waddle. Peter urged Dolly faster. The shrill of the birds became louder. A gold-feathered owl flew low, sweeping past them into the brush ahead. Far to the right Peter saw the black, humped shape of a bear loping easily along. It disappeared to the right, and Peter urged Dolly more in that direction.

Suddenly Dolly balked, and it was all he could do to control her. Then Peter froze. Not more than thirty feet away was a mountain lion. It was immense, tawny-colored, with eyes like flecks of yellow dust. Stopping in mid-stride, it watched the mule and the goat. Its head dipped almost to the ground, its long arching neck rippling with muscles. Peter put his hand over his mouth to keep from crying out, but the big cat only twitched the tip of its long tail and bolted through the timber. Dolly grew incensed. The

smell of smoke was suddenly stronger, and Peter struggled frantically with her. Finally in desperation he dismounted. Clutching her halter, he pulled and tugged her forward. But he had to walk now. Only his presence saved Dolly from becoming terrified. Tornado ran on ahead. When almost out of sight, he stopped and babbled at them to hurry, hurry, hurry.

It seemed an eternity, a lifetime, that he battled with the mule, urging her and soothing her. Peter scanned the sky overhead, hoping for a glimpse of the sun. If he could only tell his direction, catch sight of Devil's Doorstep, and somehow make his way home. But it was no use. Even in the clearing, the sun had disappeared from sight behind a heavy mass of clouds. Peter stumbled into a gopher hole and almost lost his balance. He looked overhead again. That wasn't a cover of clouds—that was smoke.

||6||

REFUGE FOR ALL

Peter, Tornado, and Dolly crossed the clearing, following the birds, the deer, and other animals. Once Peter saw a turtle slowly plodding its way, and he stopped and scooped it up in his hand. Long legs were better than short ones now, but the turtle shrank into its shell in terror.

Peter had no idea how long they traveled, or how far. Stopping now and then to settle Dolly, he watched behind them. There was still no obvious sign of the fire. Sometimes it became necessary to put the turtle down to quiet Dolly, but he always picked him up again when he urged the mule on. By now Peter was only following the dark shape of Tornado, who was bleating and bawling far ahead of them. The smoke began to hurt his nose, and pieces of charred flotsam fell from the sky like black snow.

At last they came to a meadow cut by a creek. Tornado was already splashing through the water. Peter tried to get Dolly to drink, but she was too frightened. A bear and a big elk with immense horns were dipping their heads for water. The sight sent Dolly into spasms of bucking and bolting, half-dragging Peter with her. Finally Peter wrapped his handkerchief through her halter and let it cover her eyes. If she could not see the forest things, possibly she might be quiet.

They followed the creek. "Come on, Dolly," Peter whispered into her ear. "It's all right. The water's cool. It will feel good on your feet." But Dolly was still balky. Only reluctantly did she come with Peter, and only because of his gentle, calming words. They wound along the creek bank, always in the same direction as the rush of animals.

The noise grew louder, and Peter found he was shouting to Dolly now over roars and crashes. The voice of the forest fire—the thunder of trees catching fire, the throaty belch of flames—was close behind.

"Hurry, Dolly. Oh, please hurry." Peter was almost talking to himself now. "Hurry, hurry, hurry."

Suddenly he caught up with Tornado, who had stopped and was standing in a pond formed by a beaver dam. Miraculously it still held water. Already animals were gathering there.

[91]

Peter glanced over his shoulder and saw the boil of smoke. He felt the heat of fire on his face.

He led Dolly into the deepest part of the pond. With great care and persuasion, he got her to lie down. She rolled on her side and was almost submerged. Then he, too, sank into the water and began his watch of the trees across the clearing. The smoke hurt his nose and made his eyes water and run. He took short, scorching breaths. Dolly lay quietly in the water, her head resting on Peter's shoulder, his handkerchief covering her eyes. She seemed to feel safer now and lay passively beside her friend.

It was Tornado who now became the nervous one. Peter clutched the goat and wrapped a section of shirttail around his eyes. Then Tornado, too, became quiet, submerged except for his head.

Peter did not want to look at his neighbors

in the pond. They rather frightened him, but somehow he knew these animals were not a danger. The deer and elk were lying or standing in the water; squirrels stood up to their neck. A bear nervously walked in and out, his fur plastered to his body, making him look quite small. Raccoons, hating to be wet, tried gamely to wipe themselves dry on land and yet had to reenter the water for a quick cooling. A young bobcat paced nervously back and forth on the bank, acting as though he were caged in a zoo. Almost all kinds of forest animals were there, some to stay, some to sink into the mud and slime to cool their bodies and move on. Peter wondered if he, too, should attempt to go on. But more and more animals were taking refuge in the pond, and somehow he thought it wise to stop. Dolly would balk completely now. The noise and the smoke would be too much for her. Even Tornado was nervous and upset. His little

babbles, and bleats sounded like pathetic cries of a frightened baby.

I feel like their father, thought Peter strangely. He knew that he should be afraid, for he would be lucky to come out alive. The thick, cloying smoke was the worst. He could hear the animals coughing, but they were very still. Those along the edge of the pond waded into its depths. Those in flight stopped and came back to wade ankle-deep in the water.

Peter held his nose and went under. The water felt cool and wonderful. He splashed some on Dolly's head and on Tornado's as they lay still. A doe and her fawn were lying near them, their eyes vacant with fear. Another bear ran suddenly from the trees, his black fur smoking. He plunged into the water with a great splash, then waded within a few feet of Peter, not noticing him at all.

I am just one of them, he thought. We are all

here to stay alive, natural fear and hate forgotten. A woodchuck stood on hind legs along the pool's bank. His fur was smoking, but he would not get wet. Peter wanted to go to him and throw him into the water. But he knew his friends would only become frightened if he left them.

The bear snorted beside him. Peter dipped his head and began to run his hand across his hair to see if it had burned. He found that he still held the old turtle. He dropped him into the water and watched him sink through the slime with a bubble. A snake swam by, and Peter shivered, hoping it would not come near them.

Then he saw the first sign of flame, the terrible black of new smoke. Now orange, then yellows and reds of leaping, swirling fire appeared. The flames crept along through the grass, into the brush, along the trunks of the

[97]

big pines, and, like fingers of the devil, up to the crowns. The grass around the pond suddenly burst into flame. The billowing smoke blotted out the fire in the trees, and it was dark as blackest night.

Peter coughed and splashed water on his friends. He saw the old bear sink into the water with nothing showing but the tip of his black nose. Peter sank again and again, his breath coming hot and terrible. The world about him was fogged with an orange glare. He heard the crackle and crash of thunder as trees exploded and burned around them. He felt the wind, hot as steam, touch his face. The hiss and bubble of burning pine were everywhere. A living wall of vivid fire swallowed the pond.

|| 7 ||

THE DANGER PASSES

Then, after what seemed forever, the roaring, popping, and crackling lessened. The blinding smoke turned whitish as it rose from the pond and floated overhead.

"It's past!" Peter croaked to the animals of the pond. "The fire has gone past!"

Slowly, cautiously the animals stirred. The old bear beside him erupted from the water, which sprayed from his coat like a fountain. He looked tired and stiff, his fur tipped with whit-

ish splotches of singed hair. Glancing once at
Peter, he carefully waded out to the smoking
ground. But it was still very hot. He shook his
huge paw, and then stepped back into the
water, where he stood gazing into the smoke.

The air was clearing faster now. Peter could
take great gasps into his lungs, reveling in the
knowledge that he was alive. Through the fog
of smoke the dark burned stalks of trees, standing like splinters on a black mat, were just beginning to take shape. Here and there a smoking branch crashed to the ground. Rotten logs
and old trees glowed, sending up sparks and a
sudden flare of flame, then dying and smolder-
ing their last.

The animals tenderly placed their hooves and
paws on the blackened grass around the pond,
testing for heat. A few of the elk were standing
near the water's edge. The deer and the moose
returned to cool their hooves and legs, then

moved nervously away, waiting for their chance to leave.

They would all return to their homes—burrows, nests, or meadows—only to find them gone. Many of their friends would never return. There was nothing now but desolation and ruin. What had taken hundreds of years for nature to create, took but a few hours to destroy.

The bears, raccoons, and skunks began to move. Squirrels sat along the water's edge, wet and bedraggled, looking as miserable as the land about them. Would they live through the winter now that their winter food was destroyed? Would they, and the rabbits crouching along the bank with drooping ears, find a place to live before another animal made a meal of them? Even the chipmunk was looking around helplessly. The sober beaver surveyed the very brink of doom. Without trees he would die, surely and swiftly, unless he quickly found an-

[101]

other stream and another grove of tender trees.

Peter felt a terrible unhappiness for the animals, and tears came to his eyes. Then, slowly, he took the cloth from Tornado's face. The little goat lifted his lip and babbled at him. He got to his feet more easily than Dolly, who lost her footing at first on the slippery rocks and mud. The hair on both his friends was singed. He supposed that he, too, was just as burned. His face felt hot, and his throat was sore from the touch of heat and smoke.

Peter wondered how the animals could stand the hot ground underfoot. He could feel the warmth seeping through his wet boots, and the breath of air rising from it was steaming. It did not seem to bother Dolly, but Tornado refused to step on the scorched earth.

"Silly goat," Peter said fondly. "I'll have to make you shoes." It took time to cut part of his shirt into strips, to wind them around Tornado's

[102]

feet, and to tie them securely with sections of the rope. Once finished, the goat looked peculiar, but his feet did not hurt, and he walked out of the water.

Tornado had lost his foolishness. Perhaps in that moment when the fire had been at its worst, the little goat had grown from a rattlebrained youngster to a thoughtful adult.

The three of them began to walk back the way they had come. There was no sun, but then it might easily have been getting close to dark. Walking over the blistering ground was like walking through the coals of the old wood stove in the cabin. There was no sign of life; there were no birds. The animals that had left the pond might well have disappeared from the face of the earth. The three of them could have been the only creatures left in the world. Their mountain was nowhere in sight. There was nothing but desolation.

[103]

The greens and browns of the forest had gone, leaving nothing but black. Smoke still belched from some of the taller, older trees, as if they were fighting a losing battle for each inch of their life. Beneath their feet ash puffed up in small clouds of grayish dust. It covered Peter and the wet animals in streaks of black. Dolly's pretty white coat was caked with mud and soot, and her ears rolled with each step. Behind them the great mushroom cloud of smoke still billowed into the summer sky. Peter and his friends were safe now. Even if the light wind changed and the fire turned back, it would do no damage here. There was nothing left to burn.

Peter guessed that it must be very late; it had begun to grow darker and darker. They stopped finally in a creek bed to rest. There was no water, only blackened stones, as both Tornado and Dolly found out when they dipped their heads looking for a drink. They stood exhausted, both of them drooping like wilted, dirty vegetables.

Peter took the canteen and dripped some water onto Tornado's tongue. Then he gave some to Dolly. He wasn't very successful, and possibly they didn't get any water at all, but he hoped that it would make them feel cooler. Peter suddenly felt very hungry. His lunch, which he had told Mother so long ago not to make, hovered in his mind. What he would give for it now! Then he remembered the candy bar, unwrapped it, and carefully divided it into three. He fed Dolly her piece, and she ate it stolidly. Tornado inhaled his piece and begged for more. Peter sat down on the warm stones and ate his slowly. It was terribly unappetizing, wet and soggy, tasting like a slimy pond. He threw the paper down, and it looked white and shining lying there on the blackened ground.

[107]

He was too tired to move. The animals blinked their eyes, staring at nothing.

And then, after all that had already happened that day, there came more. At first Peter, who was sitting exhausted in the stream bed, didn't really notice. He was thinking of the night he would have to spend in this oven. Already his clothes were drying and he felt as though he were being roasted. At least he would be warm.

A crash echoed across the hills. Peter jerked upright and looked up. Thick black clouds were overhead, and even as he watched lightning streaked across them while a burst of thunder followed. Then, as if cautiously testing, a raindrop fell and licked his cheek. Another touched his hand, then his arm. He could see the puff of ashes as they hit the ground. Suddenly and strangely the hot land began to steam.

"Rain!" he said unbelievingly. "It's starting

to rain!" He stood up and lifted his face to the drops. They gathered strength until it showered, then poured. His hair lay dripping across his forehead. The rain washed the ashes from Dolly's back, and she looked striped like a zebra. He shouted and began to dance in ridiculous circles, as if he had lost his senses. The rain would put out the fire! Rain! Oh, go on and rain for days and days and days!

However, once it was fully dark, and the rain kept coming steadily and thoroughly, Peter began to wish it would stop for just one moment. He was so waterlogged that he could barely move. Besides, it was getting cool. The ground had turned from hot to cold, and his only protection was Dolly. He sat dismally staring into the darkest night beneath her stomach. Tornado, smelling goaty and wet, he held in his lap. What a miserable, horrible day this had been. The only good thing was having Tornado in his arms, safe and warm, and Dolly standing solidly above him.

He knew Father and Mother were all right. The helicopter would come to take them out if the lookout was in danger. But with the oncoming of the fire Father would have been so busy that he could never have left to search for him. Peter sighed. They would be terribly worried, frantic even. It was not pleasant to know that he was causing them such concern.

During the early morning hours of the next day the rain stopped. At times Peter had half slept, too tired to keep his eyes open. After a few moments, however, he came awake with a jerk and stared back into the darkness. It would be wonderful if the fire turned out to be nothing more than an awful dream in the light of the morning sun. He could hear the faint trickle of water in the stream bed, and he knew the rain had been a heavy one. Otherwise, the mountains would not pour down their wet to the streams and creeks in the valley.

Of course, dawn brought nothing more than the burned land. If anything, it looked even worse than the evening before. The morning was crystalline clear, throwing each fallen and blackened skeleton of bush and tree into sharp focus. The huge cloud of smoke was gone and in its place was the bright blue of a clean new day. The heavens were scattered with fat little clouds that would, in time, catch on the highest needle peaks and lie in the valleys like folds of marshmallow cream.

Peter stretched his aching body. There was a rise a few miles away, and his first business of the day was to get there and look about for a sight of Devil's Doorstep. Surely one of those peaks in the distance must be it, but miles and objects were deceiving.

"Come on," he told his friends. He still held

[111]

Dolly's lead, but she was following from habit. To her one burned spot of ground looked much like another. She must leave it to Peter to find them something to eat.

Peter's own stomach was gurgling hungrily. Tornado stopped to forage a black finger of brush, but it only broke and crackled as it fell to the ground. The whole world smelled of wet ashes.

Once on the slopes of the hill Peter still could not find Devil's. The sun had to be in the east. He knew that he looked to the left when he sat at his pinnacle to watch the sunrise. The mountain, right there, the one that still stood green and fresh, must then be Devil's Doorstep. But where was the tower? He hugged Tornado to his chest. Peter hated to think that he was more lost than ever. Even with the sun for a beacon he could not find his way home. His eyes went back to the mountain. No, it simply did not look right. Surely he ought to be able to see the lookout. Perhaps he was behind the mountain, perhaps that was Devil's over there.

Tornado bleated noisily.

"I know," said Peter sharply. "I'm just as hungry as you are. No need sniffing the breeze like that. You'll only smell cooked trees." Peter let the goat free. "We can pretend, though. Pretend we smell bacon frying and coffee perking." He took a deep sigh, relishing the thought of eggs and toast.

He breathed again and again. Suddenly Tornado bolted through the wet ash and disappeared over the crest of the hill. At the same instant a wonderful, delicious smell came to Peter. It wasn't a mouth-watering dream. That smell was real.

He tugged the reluctant Dolly up the slope to the top. He could hear Tornado calling nois-

[113]

ily on the other side. Now he was back, babbling at the two laggards. Peter stumbled to the top, and looked over the loveliest sight he could ever remember having seen.

‖8‖

HOME AGAIN

There, rising up ahead of him, farther away than he had ever expected, was Devil's Doorstep. At its very summit was the tiny lookout. Endless green forest stretched out away from him as far as the eye could see. No fire had touched this section; the big stream, a short distance away, was the dividing line between black charred earth and rich fertile land.

But this scene passed from his sight in an instant. What Peter riveted his eyes upon was a

circle of men, at least twenty of them, standing about a truck parked beside the stream. Even now they were turning and looking up at him. Three helicopters sat in a clearing, and around them were parked trucks, jeeps, and so much fire-fighting paraphernalia that Peter could not

believe his eyes. From one truck was coming the smell of bacon frying. Even Dolly came to life, running down the blackened hill and plunging into the stream behind Peter and Tornado. On the other side they were all helped ashore by work weary hands.

[117]

Bill Price was there, and Peter clutched him tightly. Immediately, Bill stuffed him with food while one of the rangers called Father on the radio. The men stopped eating. Their tired, red-rimmed eyes watched Peter, with interest and admiration, as he told of his refuge in the beaver pond and of the animals that had shared it with him. Bill settled himself on the tailgate of a truck and clapped Peter on the shoulder. "We were gathering to find you," he said pleasantly. "The fire's out, and the men are coming in." No need for him to tell Peter that they had held out little hope for him. Peter already knew he had been very, very lucky.

At last Bill shook his hand and left. He had to go out one more time to scout the fire area and look for any survivors—animals or men— of the flames. Most of the others left, too, some in the trucks, some in the remaining helicopters. A few stayed behind and waved with him to the disappearing fire fighters. These men, Peter knew, were the smoke jumpers. They were a rugged breed, risking death and injury as they parachuted down to fight fires in the desolate areas. The jumpers had elected to see Peter back to the lookout. Bill Price had wanted to fly him, but Peter was responsible for getting Dolly and Tornado home to the summit.

While returning, Peter learned the fire had started, apparently, not long after he had left with Tornado. A thin-ribbon of smoke, which might have been nothing more than a camper's fire, was reported by Mr. Admundsen on Eagle's Peak. Father had thought Peter would leave Tornado quickly and return to the tower. But the trickle of smoke had been a fire in the timber, and it spread fast. Before the smoke jumpers had even left their plane, the fire had crowned and begun its horrible, sickening march down the wind.

[119]

Amid disaster, however, had come some good. Because fire weather had been approaching for many days, the fire fighters were already moving before the lookout on Eagle's Peak had put down his transmitter. Rangers, firemen, and every person who could lift a shovel were drafted into the fire-fighting team. They worked for hours on the fire lines, always in the path of the fire. The smoke jumpers with him had been the lifesaving team that kept the fire from jumping the stream into the wilderness of the Devil's Doorstep area. Other crews, miles away, kept the fire from jumping the great Canada River and spreading in the opposite direction.

Probably as Peter crouched in the pond, struggling to stay alive, the fire fighters had not been far away. But luckily he had not moved. For the men, frantic to stop the fire, had used a dangerous trick to quench it—they had backfired. Deliberately they started another fire in

[120]

the path of the main flames and made it eat its way backward. When the two fires met it was the end, for with nothing left to burn but blackened land they withered and died.

Everyone had been lucky. There had been little wind, and the fire had never become hot enough to crown and leap ahead uncontrollably. And then had come the rain, the dampening finish.

Needless to say, the family reunion later that day was joyful. Mother in her happiness all but cried. Father clapped Peter on the shoulder, slapped Dolly on the rump, and eyed Tornado with a slight glint in his eye. "Thank goodness, his hose nibbling wasn't serious," he said to Peter. They settled Dolly, famished and thirsty, in her stall. Eating like a hungry lion, she closed her eyes in contentment.

Peter sighed happily himself. Father and Mother talked to the men while they waited for

[121]

Bill Price to come back and fly them out. It had been a long climb, and everyone was tired.

Suddenly Mother screamed. Peter leaped from the porch steps, where he had been resting against Father's knee.

"Good grief!" said one of the smoke jumpers, startled.

Peter stared. A ghost! A running, weaving, waving, white ghost flew around the cabin and ran across the clearing, making strange and peculiar noises.

"Tornado!" said Peter fiercely. He ran for the animal, caught him, pulled the sheet from his back and head, and looked at him sternly.

"Well," said Mother, half-laughing. "I can imagine what the rest of my laundry must look like if he's been attacking it."

Father laughed. Peter knew it was a very good time to disappear with Tornado.

"You silly goat," said Peter. "Can't you behave for one minute?" They ran up the thousand feet to the pinnacle and settled snugly in the little special place overlooking their world.

Far, far below toward Eagle's Peak Peter saw the great black swath cut by the fire. It looked like a patch on the deep green of the forest. Someday, soon, snow would cover its ugliness, and in spring the fresh, green grass would come. Vines would grow and twine about the hulks and skeletons that were left. The forestry service would reseed, and then one day seedlings would appear and slowly grow into saplings. As the years went by, and he grew from boy to man, perhaps he would see those saplings turn into lovely, swaying trees.

It would be a long, long wait—his entire life. But he could hope. Peter ruffled Tornado's beard and grinned.

Born in Nebraska and educated in California, Marian Rumsey is a travel enthusiast. Some years ago she and her husband and two children completed a cruise around the world, which included a year's stopover in the Hawaiian Islands. Most recently they spent a great deal of time in the northwestern United States and in Canada, a country of great forests, similar to those described in *Devil's Doorstep*. They next plan to go to the South Pacific and Australia. Mrs. Rumsey is known in the boating and yachting field through the many articles she has written about the family cruises. She also writes general travel articles, in addition to her work on children's books.